SALTED CARAMEL KILLER

Cupcakes in Paradise

Book 3

By

Summer Prescott

Copyright © 2017 Summer Prescott

All rights reserved.

ISBN:9781973781165

Copyright 2017 Summer Prescott Books

All Rights Reserved. *No part of this publication nor any of the information herein may be quoted from, nor reproduced, in any form, including but not limited to: printing, scanning, photocopying, or any other printed, digital, or audio formats, without prior express written consent of the copyright holder*

**This book is a work of fiction. Any similarities to persons, living or dead, places of business, or situations past or present, is completely unintentional.

Author's note: I'd love to hear your thoughts on my books, the storylines, and anything else that you'd like to comment on—reader feedback is very important to me. My contact information, along with some other helpful links, is listed below. If you'd like to be on my list of "folks to contact" with updates, release and sales notifications, etc.… just shoot me an email and let me know. Thanks for reading!

Also…

… if you're looking for more great reads, I am proud to announce that Summer Prescott Books publishes several popular series by Cozy author Patti Benning, as well as Carolyn Q. Hunter, Blair Merrin, Susie Gayle and more! Check out my book catalog

http://summerprescottbooks.com/book-catalog/ for their delicious stories.

Contact Info for Summer Prescott:

Twitter: @summerprescott1

Blog and Book Catalog:

http://summerprescottbooks.com

Email: summer.prescott.cozies@gmail.com

And…look up The Summer Prescott Fan Page and Summer Prescott Publishing Page on Facebook – let's be friends!

To sign up for our fun and exciting newsletter, which will give you opportunities to win prizes and swag, enter contests, and be the first to know about New Releases, click here:

https://forms.aweber.com/form/02/1682036602.htm

TABLE OF CONTENTS

CHAPTER ONE 10

CHAPTER TWO 18

CHAPTER THREE 28

CHAPTER FOUR 39

CHAPTER FIVE 45

CHAPTER SIX 53

CHAPTER SEVEN 62

CHAPTER EIGHT 72

CHAPTER NINE 83

CHAPTER TEN 97

CHAPTER ELEVEN 107

CHAPTER TWELVE 116

CHAPTER THIRTEEN 127

CHAPTER FOURTEEN 142

CHAPTER FIFTEEN 147

CHAPTER SIXTEEN 155

CHAPTER SEVENTEEN 160

CHAPTER EIGHTEEN 166

SALTED CARAMEL KILLER

Cupcakes in Paradise Book 3

CHAPTER ONE

Melissa Gladstone-Beckett wasn't even aware that she was frowning as she gazed out over the water, the gentle waves lapping on the beach. The quiet beauty of the view was one of the things that had enticed her to move to the sleepy small town of Calgon, Florida, after spending her honeymoon there. A strong breeze, scented with the tang of the ocean and the faintest whiff of rain, blew wispy blonde bangs across her forehead, but she didn't notice. Her thoughts were many miles away, with her husband.

Chas Beckett was a Private Investigator, and he'd been called away to a case in Illinois. There was a thirteen year old boy missing, and Missy couldn't even imagine how depraved one would have to be to kidnap a child. Her brave hubby could potentially be dealing with some very dangerous people, and she didn't like it one bit. Sleep had eluded her since Chas had been gone, and she'd spent her sleepless nights inventing new recipes for her cupcake shop and worrying about her beloved. Sighing, she stood, brushed the sand from the seat of her capris and called to her furry babies, Toffee, the aging Golden Retriever who didn't like rain, and Bitsy, the Maltipoo who reveled in it.

Hearing the rumble of thunder in the distance, Missy headed for home, her canine companions trotting amiably alongside her. Toffee glanced warily back over her shoulder when the occasional rumble of thunder signaled the impending storm.

"It's okay, girlie," Missy soothed, reaching down to scratch behind the Golden's silky ears. "We'll get you home before the big bad raindrops attack," she grinned. Bitsy gave her an excited look, her little pink tongue out.

**

"Oooooh! Something smells amazing," Missy's best friend, Echo Kellerman cooed, shaking the raindrops from her artfully tousled mass of red curls. Her beautiful baby girl, Jasmine was snoring peacefully, secured to her mother with a wrap.

"Thanks, I'm trying out a new recipe this morning," Missy handed her friend two coffee cups and reached for a slab of butter with which she'd start her luscious frosting.

"Oh? What is it?" Echo poured both of them a cup of coffee and went over to peer through the glass in the front of the oven, her hand cupped protectively around little Jazzy's head.

"Lemon Cheesecake cupcakes. The cake itself is lemon, and it'll be filled with cheesecake. The frosting will be lemon buttercream, with a tiny bit of zest on top," Missy announced proudly, waiting for a reaction.

"Are there any vegan ones done yet?" Echo eyed the cooling rack hopefully.

"Sorry, but they're still in the oven, the tray on the left is the first vegan batch."

"Can't wait to try them, they smell delicious."

"Well, you can help me frost the ones that are ready to go, while this next batch cools, if you have time, and then we'll have a cupcake break," Missy grinned.

"I wish I could, but Joyce signed the two of us up for personal training sessions at her gym. They have a great childcare program, so I agreed to it for some strange reason," Echo sighed.

Joyce Rutledge, a dedicated bookworm, who was a force to be reckoned with, managed the book shop and adjacent candle store that Echo owned in a funky old building downtown. Just recently, the young woman had apparently embarked upon a crusade to get into the best shape of her life, which baffled Missy and Echo. Joyce was plump in all the right places, as a result of some seriously wonderful kitchen skills. She was seemingly comfortable in her own skin, so the friends wondered what was spurring on her newfound fitness craze.

Missy giggled. "Funny, I never really pictured you as the gym type."

"Hey, I wear yoga pants sometimes," Echo fired back, looking decidedly less-than-enthused about the prospect of working out.

**

Echo Kellerman felt more than a bit out of place as she entered the foyer of the gym, trying to find a place to sit and wait for Joyce.

"I think I'm the oldest person here," she mused, shifting Jazzy onto her hip and observing the taut young twenty-somethings who looked fabulous, even in their workout gear.

An extremely fit man, who looked to be somewhere in his mid-thirties and had a nose that looked like it had seen its share of bar fights, approached with a broad smile.

"You must be Mrs. Kellerman. I'm Andre Weisman, your trainer," he held out his hand and she shook it.

"Hi Andre. Bet I wasn't hard to pick out of the crowd," Echo joked self-consciously, cuddling Jazzy closer.

"Well, since I'd been told to look for a stunning redhead, no, it wasn't too hard to find you," he surprised her by saying. "Joyce is waiting for us in the training room. Let me show you where to take your adorable little girl," he said, gesturing to a doorway, which Echo hoped didn't lead to a torture room. She left Jazzy in the arms of a child-loving pro, who seemed to thrive among stuffed bunnies and blocks and primary colors, and felt confident that her daughter would enjoy time spent at the gym much more than she would.

"Hey girl," Joyce greeted Echo with a hug, jumping up from the bright purple exercise ball on which she'd been sitting. "You ready for this?" Her eyes were bright.

"No. You're fired," Echo sighed, taking in the various weights, bands and equipment neatly arranged in the room that smelled of yoga mats with a faint undertone of dirty socks.

Andre offered a hand to Joyce to help her stand up, and the coy, sassy look in the young woman's eyes told Echo everything she needed to know about why Joyce was suddenly so interested in fitness.

SUMMER PRESCOTT

CHAPTER TWO

"Ouch," Echo groaned, getting out of Missy's car in front of an upscale department store.

"You okay, darlin'?" Missy's brow furrowed with concern.

"I'll be fine," was the muttered response. "I just used muscles yesterday at the gym that I didn't even know I had."

Missy suppressed a smile. "Enjoying your personal training sessions?"

Echo shot her a look. "No. I'm doing this for Joyce. She really seems to be quite taken with our fitness instructor."

"Well good for her. Is the feeling mutual?" Missy locked the car after Echo eased herself out of it.

"Hard to say. Andre is so charming to everyone that he makes even old out-of-shape gals like me feel better."

"Well, Joyce is pretty selective, so he should consider himself lucky." Missy eyed the door of the shop in front of them. "Maybe I should just wear one of the dresses that I have at home," she sighed. "It just seems so wasteful to buy an expensive dress for one event."

"It's a gala," Echo shrugged. "You buy the dress, wear it once, then use it for out-of-town functions. That's how life works. You'd be the talk of the town if you wore a dress that's already been seen in public," she rolled her eyes.

Missy shook her head. "It just seems silly."

"It is what it is," was her friend's pragmatic reply, as she hooked her arm through Missy's and shepherded her into the store. "C'mon, it'll be fun."

The gal pals made their way back to the formal wear section of the store, where stunning gowns glittered and shimmered, and Missy's reluctance grew.

"These gowns are expensive," she whispered, catching sight of some of the price tags.

"Well, since it's for a charity function, why don't you donate the same amount of money that you spend on the gown?" Echo suggested.

Since she was married to the primary heir of the Beckett fortune, Missy didn't ever have to actually worry about money, but her attitudes toward it were the same as they had been while growing up in small-town Louisiana.

"I like that idea," she nodded, still uncertain.

"Good afternoon ladies," a cheerful voice greeted them from behind.

When they turned toward the source of the voice, Echo's eyebrows shot up in surprise. "Andre? You work here, too?" she asked the well-dressed man with the crooked nose.

"Man cannot live on muscles alone, Mrs. Kellerman," he grinned. "Who is your lovely friend?"

"This is Missy, my best friend in the whole world, and we desperately need dresses for the gala next month."

"It's a pleasure to meet you, Missy," Andre shook her hand. "I'm sure that we can find amazing dresses to complement your exquisite beauty," he appraised both women with a professional eye.

"I don't even know where to start," Missy blushed. "I'm feeling pretty overwhelmed right now," she admitted.

"Then you just have a seat right over here," he led her to a plum-colored velvet couch. "I'll have Amanda bring you some tea, and I'll bring over a selection of gowns for you to try on," he gestured to a thin young woman with black hair who was buttoning the back of a gown on a mannequin, and she nodded, disappearing.

"Oh, that's so nice of you," Missy beamed, relieved. "My size is…" she began, a bit self-conscious.

Andre raised a hand to stop her. "No worries, I think I've got this," he reassured her and set off on a hunt for gowns.

"He knows what size I am just by looking at me?" she whispered to Echo, astonished.

"We'll see how that works out," her friend was skeptical.

"Here we are, ladies," the raven-haired young woman set a silver tea tray down on the alligator patterned ottoman in front of them. "If you want sugar and cream, both are here, and the cookies just came out of the oven. Please let me know if you need anything else," she smiled and disappeared, just as Andre returned with four amazing gowns over each arm.

"I've found four for each of you to begin with. Have some tea and cookies while I put them in the dressing rooms and then we can get started."

"I could get used to this," Echo commented, after he walked away.

"I feel so spoiled. This is wonderful. No wonder Joyce has a crush on Andre," Missy bit into a cookie so warm and tender that it practically made her eyes roll back in her head. "Even if she is barking up the wrong tree."

"What do you mean?"

"Well, I think he probably has a boyfriend rather than a girlfriend, don't you think?" Missy lowered her voice.

Echo burst out laughing. "No, that's not the vibe I get at all. Men can choose formal gowns without being gay, you know."

"Of course I know that, but he just seems so knowledgeable and put-together," Missy defended herself, blushing a little bit.

"You mean like Chas?" Echo arched an eyebrow.

"Shush, here he comes," Missy patted her leg and inclined her head.

"Okay, beautiful ladies, let's go get your glam on," Andre grinned and led the way to the side-by-side fitting rooms. "Come out and show them off," he called out, after they were secured in their respective rooms.

Missy unzipped the back of a gossamer pink gown that took her breath away when she saw it. She was a bit dubious when she looked at the tag, the dress was a size smaller than what she normally wore, and she hoped that she wouldn't damage it trying to get it zipped back up. Slipping into the gown, she zipped up the zipper easily, it was a perfect fit and looked utterly gorgeous.

"Oh!" she exclaimed, turning this way and that, to take in every perspective in the mirrors.

"What?" Echo called from next door. "Come out and show me," she commanded.

"I want to see yours too."

The two women came out and stared at each other in amazement, Missy glowing in soft pink and Echo resplendent in vibrant green.

"Looks like my work here is done," Andre nodded appreciatively.

"I don't know how you did it, but you managed to choose the most perfect dresses ever," Echo was delighted, staring in the mirror.

"That color makes your eyes even more mesmerizing," Andre replied. "And Missy, you look absolutely regal in that gown."

"Why thank you, kind sir," she curtsied deeply, playing the part in order to cover her blushing.

"I don't need to try anything else on," Echo surveyed her look in the mirror, hands on hips.

"Neither do I, this was unbelievably easy. Andre, thank you so much," Missy smiled, heading back to the dressing room.

"The pleasure was mine, ladies. I'll go grab a couple of garment bags and get those wrapped for you. Just leave them hanging in the dressing room. Now, will you be needing shoes today?"

"We're women, of course we need shoes," Echo laughed, closing the fitting room door.

Half an hour later, the friends were out the door and on their way to dinner at Echo's.

"Andre really made that experience so nice, even if I'll be making a huge donation at the gala after spending such a ridiculous amount on my dress," Missy remarked.

"It's a win-win, you get a fabulous dress and the charity gets a boatload of cash. Who knew that Andre had so many talents? If Joyce does manage to land him, she'll have quite the catch," Echo agreed.

"Here's hoping," Missy held up crossed fingers and smiled.

SUMMER PRESCOTT

CHAPTER THREE

Joyce Rutledge was in a great mood. She'd lost a couple of pounds since she'd started working out with Andre, and had managed to convince him to drop by the bookstore sometime. She didn't really want to lose weight, she actually loved her ample curves, so she compensated for her extra time at the gym by having dessert a few times a week. So far it was working out well.

The first customer of the day came in as soon as she unlocked the front door. The younger brunette, who wore her hair in a ponytail and had an adorable cotton print dress on, gave Joyce a big smile when she unlocked the front door.

"Hi! I couldn't wait for you to open, I've been looking all over town for a book and I heard that you might have it," she announced, fanning herself in the late summer heat.

"Well, good morning," Joyce was delighted to see another book lover. "I hope we have it. What title are you looking for?"

"It's called, *Your Powerfully Positive Thought Life*," the young woman replied.

Joyce frowned. "Hmm…doesn't ring any bells, let's see if it's in the Self Help section," she turned and led the way. "You look really familiar…have we met somewhere?"

"I was thinking the same thing. Do you go to Shoreline Fitness?"

"Yes, I just started going there recently," Joyce nodded absently, scanning for the book.

"My boyfriend Andre is a trainer there, so I'm there all the time."

Joyce paused for a moment, her face not registering the shock that she felt inside. "That must be where I've seen you then. Andre is my trainer."

"Isn't he just the best? Don't get discouraged with your progress, I've seen him work miracles, it'll just take a bit of time," she meant to be reassuring, but her comment rankled.

"I'm actually more than pleased with my progress," Joyce replied, sounding much calmer than she felt. She wasn't overly upset that Andre was taken, but she was astonished that he was with this wisp of a girl who had just insulted her.

"Oh that's so great! A positive attitude is so important," the girl nodded.

"Seems as though we don't have the book you're looking for," Joyce turned around, pasting on a plastic smile. "I'd be happy to order it for you."

"Oh no, that's okay. I'll just get it online, it'll be cheaper."

"There's certainly something to be said for purchasing from local businesses," Joyce gave her a pointed look.

"Oh absolutely," the young woman's smile didn't quite reach her eyes. "I always try to do that. Have a great day," she turned and left with a swish of her cutesy cotton dress and Joyce frowned.

"Well, if that's what works for him, he wouldn't appreciate my fine wit and Ivy League education anyway," she mused, with a sassy head tilt and pursing of the lips.

**

Missy and Echo were enjoying a cup of coffee and cupcakes at Cupcakes in Paradise, Missy's cozy little shop by the beach, with Jasmine sleeping soundly in her baby seat at their feet, when the front door opened.

"Hi all!" Andre waved as he came in.

"What on earth are you doing here?" Echo teased. "I would think this would be the last place I'd ever see you. Don't you turn to dust at the sight of sugar?"

Andre and Missy chuckled.

"No ma'am, I enjoy a good cupcake on special occasions, but I'm not shopping for myself today. Missy, when you told me that you had a cupcake shop, it made me think of Joyce. She's been working so hard at the gym and I know that she loves her dessert, so I thought I'd surprise her. She invited me to come take a look at the bookstore and candle shop, and I didn't want to come empty-handed," he explained.

"Looking for a book?" Echo waggled her eyebrows comically.

"Actually, I collect candles, and Joyce tells me that your handmade ones are exquisite," he didn't miss a beat.

"Speaking of which," Echo looked at her watch, "I need to get going so that I can help Joyce open up," she said, stuffing the last bite of cupcake in her mouth.

"Watch out, that's ten more minutes on the treadmill later," Andre's mouth twitched when Echo gave him a mock-scathing glance before heading out the door.

"You two," Missy shook her head and moved behind the counter. "Now, for some cupcakes for Joyce…"

**

Echo's phone rang and she was surprised to see that it was her husband, Kel, calling. The world-renowned, but locally raised, artist had been hard at work on his latest sculpture when she'd left, and had barely registered her kiss goodbye because he was so immersed in his project. She didn't think she'd be hearing from him until well after she got home from the candle shop.

"Hey handsome, are you calling to ask me out to lunch?" she answered cheerfully.

There was a pause before Kel answered. "Sadly, no. Were you working in your studio before you left this morning?"

"No. I finished up a batch of candles last night and didn't go in there at all this morning…why?" her stomach dropped at her husband's somber tone.

"The whole room is flooded. The water taps were left on at full blast, and every bit of furniture, all of the drywall, and the flooring is ruined."

"That's impossible. I didn't even use the sink last night, other than to get a glass of water while I worked, but I know I turned off the tap," Echo's heart sank. Her studio was at the back of their contemporary home and was one of her favorite places on earth. It had floor to ceiling windows with unique angles, and had been floored in bamboo. The thought that someone had violated her privacy and ruined her sanctuary chilled her to the bone.

"Did you see anything on the cameras?"

"I turned the security off, since I knew I was going to be home all day. It may have even happened last night," Kel sighed. "Are you absolutely certain that you didn't leave the water on?"

"Positive. Without a doubt," Echo was heartsick.

"Okay then, I'll give the police a call. I doubt that there's anything that they'll be able to do, but I'll give it a shot. I'm so sorry that this happened, my love."

"Me too," tears welled in Echo's eyes as she hung up.

"What's wrong?" Joyce read her boss's face instantly when Echo walked over to the bookstore half of the building.

Echo related her call with Kel.

"Okay, you just need to go," Joyce squeezed her arm. "I've got this. We're not too busy today anyway. Go take care of business, girl. Go on," she shooed Echo away. "And you let me know if you need anything," she called after her boss.

"You're the best, Joyce," Echo's voice was tremulous as she hurried toward the candle shop.

**

"Hey! You finally decided to come see the store," Joyce exclaimed when Andre walked in.

"You didn't leave me much choice," he grinned, handing her the box of cupcakes that Missy had helped him select. "For you, because you've been working so hard."

"Cupcakes from a trainer?" she looked at him suspiciously. "Are they like protein-packed, low carb, gluten free cupcakes?" her eyes narrowed.

Andre held up his hands in self-defense, laughing. "I'm thinking that you'd never let me get away with something like that. Nope, these are the real thing. Missy helped me pick out her best ones, I swear."

"Trying to fatten me up so I'll have to buy more training sessions?" she teased.

"Whatever works," he flirted.

Before Joyce could respond, a shrill sound ululated through the building, piercing their eardrums with its intensity.

"It's the alarm," Joyce yelled, above the din. "I have to go check the back door. I'll be right back."

She ran to the back of the store, and found the back door open maybe an inch. She hit the button to silence the alarm, then punched in the code so that their security agency wouldn't send a team. Going out the back, she looked in every direction and saw no one. Frowning, she locked the back door, making sure that it was dead-bolted, reset the alarm, and headed back to the front. Andre was nowhere to be found, and one of her cupcakes was missing.

"This must just be the day for weird stuff happening," she shook her head and went back to work, reviewing the inventory slips from the shipment that had come in yesterday.

Scanning the list, she laughed out loud. "Psssh, wouldn't you just know it…three copies of *Your Powerfully Positive Thought Life*."

CHAPTER FOUR

Joyce Rutledge was halfway through her second Salted Caramel cupcake when she heard a strange sound outside her window. Thinking that a neighbor's cat must be out prowling among her trash cans, she dismissed the sound, absorbed in her latest mystery novel. One of the main perks of working in a bookstore was having access to all of the latest books. That, and the fact that her entire house smelled amazing because she had one or more of Echo's candles in every room.

When she heard the sound again, she licked her fingers, put down her book and slipped her feet into her house slippers. Determined to discover once and for all just what was going on outside, she marched around the side of her rented house, illuminating her path with the flashlight on her cell phone. There was a rustling of leaves in the large bush next to her neighbor's house, but when she shone her beam on it, she saw nothing but some leaves quivering.

"Hmm…those leaves are pretty high up to have been moved by a stray cat," she mused, wondering whether or not to get closer to the bush. Her decision was made for her when the lights in her house suddenly went out. Trying not to panic, Joyce jogged to the neighbor's front door, and rang the bell twice.

"Alright already!" a cranky voice called out from behind the door. "I ain't deaf, I heard you the first time."

Joyce's ninety year old neighbor, whom she referred to in her mind as "Old Lady Asterly," opened the door and glared out at her.

"Whatever you're selling, I ain't buying," she snapped, squinting to see, despite her thick glasses. "Do you know what time it is, young lady?" she shook a gnarled finger at Joyce.

"Yes, Mrs. Asterly, it's 9:35," Joyce sighed. "I think someone may be playing a prank on me, so I don't want to go back into my house. May I come in for just a moment, so that I can call the police?"

"Police? I don't want to be involved," the old woman started to shut the door, but Joyce stuck her foot it in.

"Mrs. Asterly, please. You won't be involved in anything, just let me sit inside with you for a few minutes, please," Joyce said firmly, clearly not willing to take no for an answer.

"Darn kids these days, keeping me up all night," the geriatric neighbor grumbled, standing back to let Joyce in. "I s'pose you expect me to make you some tea, too."

"No, I don't expect that at all," Joyce sighed, pushing the buttons for 911 on her phone.

"Fine. I'll go put the kettle on, just sit here and hold your horses," Mrs. Asterly commanded, pulling the two halves of her worn robe together and tying the belt more tightly.

**

"Well, Ms. Rutledge, I don't see any evidence of forced entry. Were your doors locked while you were outside?" the uniformed cop asked her.

"No, I left the front door unlocked when I went outside so that I could get back in, but whoever it was would've had to have been really fast to get in while I was beside the house. The lights went out right after I got outside," Joyce shook her head, befuddled.

"Your breaker switch had been thrown, almost as though you'd put too heavy a load on your electrical circuits. Were you using a computer or anything before you left? Personal air conditioner unit, maybe?" he asked.

"Nope, I was just sitting there, reading my book and having a cupcake. I heard a funny noise, went outside, and saw the bushes behind the house, by the neighbor on the other side, rustling. Then the lights went out and I came over to Mrs. Asterly's."

"I see," the cop nodded, taking notes. "Well, unfortunately, since there's no sign of breaking in, and the electrical issue may have just been a surge or something, there's not much that I can do for you. I wouldn't worry too much about it. It may have just been some kids on a dare," he reassured her. "Lock your windows and doors and have a good night. Call us if anything else happens," he advised.

"Okay, I will. Thank you," Joyce replied, troubled.

The police officer left, and she did as he suggested, but still felt uncomfortable. First, the alarm had gone off at work, now this. She wasn't a big believer in coincidences, and was wondering what might happen next.

"Mama always said that bad things happen in threes," she whispered, going around the house, checking behind curtain panels and in the shower, even though Calgon's finest had just done the same thing. "What next?"

CHAPTER FIVE

Echo woke early, to the sound of large trucks rumbling up the driveway. The cleanup crew had arrived to start working on demolition and restoration in her studio. While her candle-making supplies were safe, the rest of the room was a total loss, and she'd be unable to work there until the space was redone.

"I should go help them," she murmured, sitting up in bed.

"No, you should go get Jazzy dressed and fed so that you don't miss your appointment at the gym," Kel encouraged, rubbing her lower back as he lay beside her.

"I'm sure he'll understand…" she began to protest.

"Beloved, don't worry about things here. The pros have the renovation well in hand, let's leave the work to them. You go meet Joyce and let Jazzy have her recreation time at the gym. It'll be good for you and it'll take your mind off of what's going on here," her husband advised, his voice gentle and sleepy.

"I suppose," Echo sighed and laid her head on her knees, which were drawn up to her chest.

"And then go see Missy. Just take a day for yourself and don't worry. It'll all be taken care of, I promise."

"But how did this even happen?" she worried.

"What's done is done. We'll get past this."

"Okay," Echo's voice was uncertain.

"Trust me, my beautiful wife. Soon this will all be a distant memory and you'll be back making candles in no time."

**

"Hey," Echo greeted Joyce with a hug, after dropping Jazz off at the childcare room at the gym. "You look tired…everything okay?"

"I'll tell you later," Joyce didn't seem to be her typical sassy self. "You look like you had a rough night too," she observed, eyeing the lines around Echo's eyes and mouth.

"Yeah, kinda."

A man with a perfect flat-top haircut, a flawless complexion and a killer smile approached them just then.

"Hello," he said, with a compelling Australian accent. "Are you Echo and Joyce?"

"Yes," they answered in unison, making the Aussie chuckle.

"Well, great to meet you both, I'm Simon, and I'm filling in for your trainer this morning. I've gone over the notes, so if you're ready to get to work…" he gestured toward the training room with a smile.

"Wait, where's Andre?" Joyce asked, her heart beating faster.

"I don't know, actually. He may have called in sick or something," Simon shrugged. "But I can assure you, I'll be every bit as attentive as he was. Shall we?" he turned and headed into the room. Joyce and Echo exchanged a curious glance and followed.

The new trainer worked them hard, but was very pleasant, letting them rest a bit between sets so that they didn't feel nearly as worn out after their workout. He chatted with them during their intervals, and it was a bit of a surprise to find out that he loved working with rescue animals, and he'd studied botany and landscape design in Australia. Brawn and brains mixed with philanthropy made a delightful substitute for the ever-charming Andre.

After thanking the new trainer with the sexy accent, they headed for the locker room, feeling tired but not exhausted. Echo showered and dressed, then headed for the childcare room. Joyce took a bit longer, luxuriating in the stinging spray of the shower. When she finished dressing, putting on her makeup and getting ready to go open the shop, she came out of the locker room and saw a contingent of policemen at the front desk. When she moved toward a side door, so that she didn't interrupt whatever was going on, they surged toward her, a rumpled detective in a bad polyester suit leading the way.

"Joyce Rutledge?" the detective called out, causing others in the gym to look over and see what was happening, much to her consternation.

"Yes," she frowned, wondering why a policeman would be asking for her, and contemptuous of the fact that he'd done it in such a less-than-subtle way. "Did you find out who cut off my power last night?" she asked, the potential reason for the police visit finally dawning on her.

"I don't know anything about that," the detective approached, eyeing her suspiciously. "I find that paying my bill on time usually helps."

"How dare you?" Joyce was outraged. "You don't know anything about me and you're just assuming that I don't pay my bills?"

She shook her head in disbelief, and moved to brush past the detective, but he stopped her.

"Not so fast. You're coming to the station with me," he caught her by the arm.

"First, I'm not going anywhere with anyone until I find out just exactly what is going on here, and second, don't you ever think you can put your hands on me without my permission, because I'm not having that," she raised an eyebrow at him and looked down at his hand on her arm. "I don't even know who you are."

He dropped his hand with a sour look on his face. "Detective Arthur Solinsky, Calgon PD, Homicide Division. Look, you can make this easy on yourself and come with me, or I can arrest you for impeding my investigation," he shrugged. "Leave willingly, or leave in handcuffs, it's entirely up to you."

"Homicide?" Joyce was startled.

"Yeah, Homicide. You coming with me or what?"

"Who was…?" she couldn't bring herself to finish the rest of the question.

"You ain't asking the questions here, I am," Solinsky's profound Jersey accent grated on her nerves, but she nodded numbly.

"Fine," her mouth compressed into a thin line. "Just let me get my car and I'll meet you at the police station."

"Your car has already been impounded and is being searched for evidence."

CHAPTER SIX

Mortician and Calgon Coroner, Timothy Eckels, snapped on a pair of blue nitrile gloves so that he could do a brief examination of the deceased before zipping him into a body bag and whisking him away to the morgue, where a full autopsy would be performed. He and his mortuary tech had already photographed the body from multiple angles and had taken notes and measurements of the scene.

"That's not a heart attack, is it?" his dark-haired Tech, Fiona McCamish, muttered from beside him.

He shot her a reproving look from behind his coke-bottle thick lenses. One of his steadfast rules was that they never discussed the deceased at the scene, where police and bystanders might read too much into their comments. He also never gave opinions or made initial assessments on site, particularly since the new homicide detective had been hired. To say that Tim Eckels and Art Solinsky didn't see eye to eye would be more than an understatement.

"How long is this gonna take, Eckels?" Detective Solinsky growled, as Timothy knelt by the body, which had been found in the alley behind his former neighbor's bookstore and candle shop.

"Much longer if I continue to have interruptions," Tim replied mildly, his gaze unwavering in the face of the detective's hostile stare.

"Then get on with it, and give me a preliminary report before you leave," Solinsky barked.

"No," Tim said quietly, lifting one of the corpse's eyelids.

"What do you mean, no?" the detective's voice was a bit menacing, and highly annoyed.

Tim pushed his glasses up with the back of his wrist, which Fiona recognized as a sign that her mild-mannered and eccentric boss was getting agitated.

"I'm fairly certain that there is only one meaning to that word, but you can look it up to make sure. My work is precise and I will not be rushed, nor will I make guesses just for your convenience. You'll have my full report just as soon as I can get it to you."

With that, Tim turned his back on an infuriated Art Solinsky, and began the meticulous process of discovering whatever story the body in front of him had to tell. Solinsky left in a huff, which Tim considered a victory. He worked better without incompetent policemen looking over his shoulder and asking pesky questions.

When the initial examination was complete, Tim and Fiona secured the deceased in a somber black body bag, and loaded him into a hearse for transport to the morgue. The two of them were silent, until Fiona's curiosity got the best of her.

"It was poison, wasn't it?" she guessed.

Fiona McCamish had a peculiar knack for mortuary work and forensics, and found her job to be an endless source of fascination. She'd had to wear Tim down, relentlessly badgering him until he hired her, despite her lack of experience. He'd made her get rid of multiple piercings and her extreme makeup and hairstyle, and had mandated that she have a professional wardrobe, rather than baggy black jeans and heavy metal t-shirts, not because he personally disapproved, but because he hadn't wanted her to "scare" potential clients with her outward signs of what looked like personal darkness. She'd complied with his requirements, and had turned out to be the best assistant he'd ever had, despite her lack of formal training.

"Of course it was," Tim commented, his eyes never leaving the road.

"Now you just have to figure out what kind?"

"That's the usual procedure, yes."

"He was actually pretty cute," Fiona mused.

"It's not right to speak about the deceased like that."

"Why? It's just a fact," Fiona challenged, enjoying her boss's discomfort. She definitely delighted in pushing Tim's buttons.

He surprised her by agreeing. "Point taken. His looks may indeed have something to do with the crime that was committed. We'll keep that in mind during the autopsy."

"Crime of passion?" she persisted in her effort to try and rattle him.

Tim gave her a sidelong glance and ignored her question.

"You know that I like you," she said abruptly, changing the subject.

Tim stared straight ahead, saying nothing.

"And I know that you like me. I can tell, even if you pretend to have no emotions," she continued, challenging him.

He didn't look at her.

"Right?" she prodded.

"You're being entirely inappropriate," Tim muttered, his jaw set.

"This isn't going to go away just because you don't want to deal with it," Fiona pointed out.

The two had been working together for a very long time. Tim was older, paunchy and pasty, Fiona was young, tough and bold, and was inexplicably drawn to her reclusive boss. She'd been around him long enough to see through the walls that he'd built around himself, where he hid from the world. They had that in common, she'd built her walls too.

"There is nothing to deal with. I am your employer, you are my employee, that is the nature of our relationship."

"Oh come on, you know that I'm more important to you than that. I'm your right arm, your trusted assistant, and you love my scintillating conversational abilities and sense of humor," Fiona smiled devilishly. Tim's continued rejection of her stung, but she knew he had some pretty deep wounds, so she persisted.

"I have no sense of humor. I work, I eat, I sleep. That is my life, that is what I understand, that is what makes me comfortable. I have no room in that formula for complications."

"You did once," she shot back, knowing that she'd gone too far the moment the words were out of her mouth.

Tim glanced away from the road briefly, just long enough to shoot Fiona a scathing glance. He never talked about his failed marriage, and never tolerated it well when someone else brought it up. The fact that he'd been married to the most notorious female serial killer ever may have something to do with that. After stopping in town for a few weeks, just a short time ago, to make an attempt on Fiona's life, simply because she worked closely with Tim, his former wife, to whom he was still legally married, had killed a few people, then fled to avoid prosecution.

"I'm sorry," she whispered, putting her hands over her mouth and shaking her head. "I didn't mean to…"

"You should invest in a car," was his terse reply.

The two carpooled every day because they were next-door neighbors. It had been an arrangement that worked for both of them.

Fiona's eyes flashed fire. "Oh, that's how it is? I accidentally blurt out something stupid, so you kick me out of the car? How neighborly of you," she challenged, so angry that she hadn't even realized that he'd pulled up in front of the morgue.

"We're here," he said simply, not looking at her.

"Someday, you're going to have to deal with this, you know. Someday you're going to have to allow yourself to be a human being who has feelings and thoughts and maybe considers sharing them with someone else, or your whole world is going to come crashing down and no one will be there," her eyes filled with tears.

"My world came crashing down a long time ago," Tim's reply was weary. "Let's get the deceased in the cooler."

Fiona got out without another word.

CHAPTER SEVEN

"Andre is dead?" Joyce was astonished, and her eyes welled a bit. "But he was so nice. Who would do such a thing?"

"That's what we'd like to know," Art Solinsky drilled her with a glare. "You're classified as a person of interest in this case at the moment, but I have to tell you, Ms. Rutledge, the physical evidence against you is mounting."

"Physical evidence? How can there be physical evidence against me? Andre was my trainer, that's it!" the young woman protested.

"So you deny the eyewitness reports which indicate that he stopped by your place of employment to visit you?"

"Eyewitness…what? No, of course I don't deny that, but it was no big deal. He said that he really likes candles, so he came by the candle store."

"There was also evidence found in his apartment and in your car. How do you explain that?" Solinsky leaned over the table toward her, and she could smell his breath, which had been away from a toothbrush for a few hours too long.

"I have no idea," Joyce shook her head, terrified rather than defiant now. "I've never been to his house, he's never been to mine, and he's never been in my car. I think you must have me confused with someone else."

"A search warrant is being drawn up right now for me to search your house. It'd be in your best interest to tell me what I might find there," Solinsky's eyes narrowed.

"You won't find anything there. This is ridiculous. I didn't even know that Andre was dead, how could I possibly be involved?"

"Not gonna cooperate, huh? Well, mark my words, we'll find out just how you were involved. I've got all night, sweetheart," the detective leaned back in his chair and laced his fingers behind his head, patches of sour sweat showing under his arms.

Joyce's fear turned into indignation. "Now let me tell you something," she bristled. "You've got the wrong person sitting in here talking to you, and you have no right to treat me like a common criminal. I am not your sweetheart, and I did not have anything to do with this. You either charge me with something, or let me go, because I'm done being subjected to your rudeness," she crossed her arms and stared at him.

There was a knock on the door to the interrogation room and a uniformed cop, coincidentally the one who had checked out Joyce's house when the power had gone out, stuck his head inside.

"Detective, I got a woman out front who's making a big stink about needing to talk to you right now.

"Well, ain't this my lucky day. Get rid of her, tell her to make an appointment," Solinsky brushed him off.

"She's this lady's boss," he gestured to Joyce. "And from what I can tell, she's not going anywhere until she talks to you."

"Well, if you can't get rid of her, I can," the detective tossed his pen down on the table and stood, bracing his lower back with his hands. He turned to Joyce before leaving the room. "You, sit there and think about telling the truth when I get back," he commanded.

"Don't you dare talk down to me," Joyce arched an eyebrow at him.

Solinsky's muttered reply as he left the room was thankfully unintelligible.

**

Echo Kellerman was beyond upset. The thought of sweet, sassy Joyce being interrogated gave her chills. She'd gone back to the gym after realizing that she'd left one of Jazzy's toys in the baby room, and one of the receptionists filled her in on what had happened between Joyce and

Solinsky. Now she was determined to find out what was going on.

"I don't care if you're in the middle of something, this is important, and if you won't take me to your office to discuss it, I'll shout it at your back as you walk away. You need to hear this. Am I making myself fairly clear?" The normally laid-back Echo was adamant.

Solinsky's jaw muscles worked as he considered what to do with the woman in front of him. He wasn't getting anywhere with Joyce, so he figured he'd let her cool her heels in interrogation for a bit while he listened to whatever rant her nut-job boss had in store for him.

"You got five minutes, follow me," he turned on his heel and strode toward the office that Chas Beckett had occupied before him. Echo vehemently wished that he still did, and felt a pang of disappointment when she saw the condition of the formerly spotless office. "Spill it," Solinsky commanded, shutting the door.

Echo stared at him, considering whether or not to give him a good tongue-lashing for his boorishness, but decided against it, in the interest of getting Joyce out of interrogation.

"I have a police report on file which tells of an incident at my home two days ago. Someone broke in and turned on the water, ruining my entire studio," she began.

"How do you know that they broke in? Is there evidence of that?" he interrupted.

"Well, no, but obviously someone did," she tried again.

"And you've never forgotten to turn the water off? Ever?"

"I'm telling you that this…"

"Do you have anything relevant to say? Because so far, this ain't cutting it," Solinsky sighed, drumming his fingers on the desk.

"Last night Joyce's home was broken into," Echo tried to clamp down on her temper, for Joyce's sake.

"Again, no evidence of that. She left the front door open for crying out loud. Probably just a stunt staged to try and throw us off while she got ready to go commit murder."

"That's utterly preposterous! This is an intelligent, well-educated woman, who…"

"Honey, I don't care if she's the queen of England, she shouldn't have killed a guy and been so sloppy about it. I got evidence all over the place. Now, if you'll excuse me," Solinsky stood.

"Don't you dare dismiss me," Echo ground out, teeth clenched. "What about the girlfriend? Have you even talked to her?"

That gave Solinsky pause. He hadn't heard about a girlfriend.

"What's her name?" he asked, still standing behind his desk.

"Well, I…actually don't know," Echo faltered.

"What's she look like?" Solinsky's expression was heavily laced with skepticism.

"Well, I haven't seen her, but Joyce says that she's young and brunette and wears her hair in a ponytail."

"So the person of interest points a finger at an unknown woman who might be the girlfriend of the deceased, and you think that changes everything? Quit wasting my time lady. It's only a matter of time before we make an arrest. This case is textbook," Solinsky headed for the door, gesturing for Echo to leave.

"Things are rarely as they seem, Detective," was the icy reply.

"Keep talking like that and I'll have to start questioning you too," he threatened, having had enough. He was going to be wickedly late for his dinner as it was, and this woman had delayed him even further.

"It would make just about as much sense," Echo huffed, brushing past him and holding her breath a bit, so as not to take in his faintly stale body odor. "You haven't heard the last of this," she tossed back over her shoulder as she made her way back to the reception desk.

"Have a nice day," Solinsky's voice dripped with sarcasm and contempt.

Busy-body citizens were the bane of his existence, and now he had to go back and question a young woman who had been less than cooperative. Popping two antacids off of a roll in his pocket, he tossed them in his mouth and crunched on them.

CHAPTER EIGHT

Missy was having a great day. She'd finally had a good night's sleep, after having indulged in a glass of wine and a good book. She had gotten up early to take the dogs for a long walk on the beach, and was headed to Cupcakes in Paradise to craft some new cupcake recipes that she'd dreamed up on her walk. She'd missed a call from Echo early this morning, but figured she'd just catch up with her when she came in before opening for coffee and cupcakes.

When she approached the back door of her shop, she knew instantly that something was wrong. The door was ajar, perhaps half an inch.

"Oh no. Why did this happen when Chas is gone?" she whispered to herself, her heart racing.

She stood outside, wondering whether or not to go in, and since she was alone in the semi-dark of sunrise, she opted to refrain from entering her cozy little shop, afraid of what…or whom, she might encounter inside. Walking quickly to the nearby bed and breakfast, which she and her husband had once owned, she let herself inside the foyer and dialed 911. She tried calling Echo once the police were on their way, but strangely, got no answer.

**

"Fortunately, there's no sign of damage or theft, Mrs. Beckett," the lantern-jawed policeman reassured her.

"Thanks Joe, I appreciate you coming out and taking a look around. Can I get you some coffee and a cupcake or two before you go?" Missy replied, relieved and puzzled.

She knew for a fact that she had locked and closed the door to the shop when she left the day before.

"Don't mind if I do. My wife raves about your cupcakes. Says they're the best in town," he grinned, taking a seat at one of the bistro tables.

"Then I'll box some up for you to take to her when you go."

"I appreciate it," Joe nodded.

The officer had just taken a bite of a cupcake, when a call came into his earpiece, and he put a hand on it, so that he could hear more clearly. He stared at the cupcake in his hand, put it down, and a very strange look crossed his features. He spoke in a voice that Missy didn't hear, into his mouthpiece, and looked up to where she was brewing another pot of coffee. The investigation had put her behind schedule, so she was going to have to keep one eye on the front of the shop, while attempting to get more cupcakes into the ovens in the back.

"Mrs. Beckett?"

"Yes, Joe?"

"I'm going to have to ask you to come down to the station with me for questioning," was the apologetic reply.

"Questioning? About what?" Missy frowned.

"The murder of Andre Weisman."

**

Timothy Eckels was elbows deep into his autopsy, and was, uncharacteristically, more confused than ever.

"We're going to have to wait for lab results on this one," he muttered to himself, shaking his head.

Fiona, who had ridden to work with him this morning, just like she did every other morning, shone her light into the abdominal cavity and peered more closely.

"Well, you still think that it's poison, right?" she asked, leaning in.

"It would appear so, despite the fact that the body tells a conflicting story," Tim mused.

"What's not adding up?" Fiona wondered, never failing to be impressed by her boss's deductive insights.

"Well, the suspected instrument of delivery isn't present in the stomach contents, to start."

"So, they're blaming the cupcake that they found at the scene, but he didn't eat the cupcake?" she translated.

"Essentially, yes."

"Could he have licked the frosting or something? There was a bite missing from the cupcake…maybe he tasted it and spit it out?" she theorized.

"That sort of speculation will get us nowhere. I would imagine that the cupcake was a decoy. There had to have been another, more intense delivery system, based upon the physiological state of the deceased," Tim's brow furrowed as he continued to probe and examine. "There's also the matter of the contusion on his head, which matched up to hair and skin samples found on the brick wall in the alley."

"He wouldn't have bruised if the impact had been made after death, like if someone had planted the body there, so he was still alive while he was in the alley," Fiona stared off into space, thinking through the implications.

"Exactly. We have an approximate time of death, based upon morbidity and all the usual markers, but we don't know how soon after the deceased either was pushed, or fell, that he died. I'll need to look at his brain."

"Why?"

"To see if seizures were involved. I have a hunch."

"Care to elaborate?" Fiona blinked at him.

"No. Too early yet. Get me ten small specimen packets," he waved her off.

"Fingernail scrapings?" she guessed, hurrying toward the supply cabinet.

"Precisely. I'll need a slide too. There's a smear on the neck that is far too pink to be blood."

**

"Do you recognize this, Mrs. Beckett?" Detective Art Solinsky seemed to hate even saying her name, as he held up an evidence baggie with a cupcake in it.

"That looks like a cupcake from my shop," Missy's eyes grew wide. "It has the paper with my logo on it, and looks exactly like the Salted Caramel cupcakes that I baked yesterday and the day before."

"Mrs. Beckett, did you interact with a Mr. Andre Weisman at Chez Vogue department store two days ago?"

"I don't know if Weisman is his last name, but yes, I met a very nice man named Andre there and bought a dress and shoes from him," Missy nodded.

"Then did you sell him some cupcakes from your shop yesterday?"

"Oh no, he told me that they were for a mutual friend, so I didn't charge him for the cupcakes."

"You just gave them to him?"

"Yes."

"Are you in the habit of giving away your cupcakes?"

"Certainly, when friends are involved."

"And just who was this mutual friend that he was getting cupcakes for?"

"Joyce Rutledge. She's a delightful gal, who…" Missy began, only to be interrupted by the detective.

"I'm acquainted with Ms. Rutledge. Are you aware of the relationship between Ms. Rutledge and Mr. Weisman?"

"Andre was Joyce's trainer."

"And are you expecting me to believe that a trainer would bring cupcakes to one of his clients?" Solinsky raised an eyebrow.

"Well, Joyce isn't a typical client. She loves her dessert, and loves her body just the way that it is."

"Then why would she take on the expense of hiring a trainer?"

"I have no idea. I do think she had a bit of a crush on him though."

"Did she say that?"

"I don't know, I just heard it from Echo. She's my friend who is Joyce's boss," Missy explained, trying to be helpful.

"Hell hath no fury…" Solinsky muttered under his breath.

"I'm sorry, what?" Missy asked, not having heard him.

"Nothing. You had a break-in of some sort this morning?"

"Yes, some officers came out and took a look around, but didn't find anything."

"Seems to be a lot of that happening lately," Solinsky stared her down.

"I don't understand," Missy frowned, not looking away, despite the somewhat hostile-seeming nature of his gaze.

"You had a "break-in" with no evidence of someone actually breaking in, your friend Echo had a similar situation, as did Joyce Rutledge. You'd think that the three of you could have planned out something a bit more original to set the stage."

"Set the stage? What are you talking about, Detective?"

"I don't know why, or how, the three of you managed to kill Andre Weisman, but I'm going to find out," Solinsky said, standing. "We're done here. For now. My guys aren't quite done investigating your "break-in" yet, so I'd advise you to just go on home and not interfere with their work."

"You can't search my shop without a warrant." Missy didn't appreciate the detective's tone or his insinuations.

"No one said anything about a search," Solinsky gave her an oily grin. "We're investigating your break-in call. If we collect evidence that may be valuable in solving who broke in, that's a good thing, right?"

"You're a sorry excuse for a detective," Missy's look was venomous. "This isn't the end of this," she said in a low voice.

"It certainly isn't. At the end of this, you and your snooty little friends will most likely be in jail. Don't leave town anytime soon, Mrs. Beckett. We'll be talking again real soon," Solinsky sneered and gestured for her to leave.

Missy snatched up her purse, shot him a scathing look and walked slowly to the door. "Your career just ended," she said quietly, as the smug look on his face slipped away.

CHAPTER NINE

"Did you talk to Chas?" Echo asked Missy as they sipped coffee in the cupcake shop, both trying to recover from their experiences with Detective Art Solinsky.

Missy nodded. "He feels like they may be getting close to resolving the case in Illinois, so he can't break away right now," she sighed, wrapping her hands around her cup and shivering a bit, despite the warmth of the Florida morning.

"Then we'll have to take care of this mess ourselves," Echo's mouth set in a determined line.

"But where do we start? Who on earth would kill Andre and set you, me and Joyce up to take the blame for it? I don't have any enemies, do you?"

"Not that I know of, but Joyce does."

"How is that even possible? She's wonderful."

"Yes, she is, and that's the problem," Echo mused regretfully.

"How do you mean?"

"I'd bet dollars to donuts that the killer is Andre's girlfriend. She probably saw the way that Joyce and Andre interacted at the gym and got jealous."

"But, assuming that she was crazy enough to kill someone out of jealousy, wouldn't she just kill Joyce, rather than her own boyfriend?" Missy pointed out.

"Maybe Joyce is next," Echo's words were chilling.

"Maybe we all are. What better way to close an investigation for murder than by making the suspects disappear?" Missy shuddered.

"Persons of interest. If we were suspects, we'd be in jail right now," Echo corrected absently, lost in thought.

"If Solinsky had his way, we all would be," Missy's lip curled at the thought of the detective. "So, how do we find out who the girlfriend is?"

"The trainer who stood in for Andre seemed very nice. Maybe if Joyce and I flirt with him, he'll tell us who she is."

"If he knows."

"Gyms are like little gossip centers. Everybody knows everybody's business. He'll know," Echo was confident.

"Well, it's worth a shot, but then what?"

"We can have Kel start asking around about her, because he knows everyone, and if we do it, it'll look suspicious. In the meantime, we can have Chas's hacker dude looking into her records. He's pretty much sitting around the office doing nothing since Chas and Spencer are in Illinois, right?"

"I have no idea what Ringo does with his down-time. Chas says sometimes he works until three a.m., then shuts the door and sleeps in the office during the day," Missy made a face. The eccentric young man had always baffled her.

He was a genius, and very helpful, but had no social skills whatsoever.

"Well, we'll bring him a pizza and a six pack of cola and he'll be like putty in our hands," Echo smiled faintly.

"I suppose it's worth a shot. At least until we can find something more to go on," Missy sighed.

"You should eat something," Echo said softly, taking in her friend's weary look.

"It all tastes like sawdust right now. I'm going to go do some baking. Let me know what you and Joyce find out from the new trainer."

"Will do. Do you want to stay with me tonight?"

"While I'd like to, I think it might just add fuel to Solinsky's fire and make him think that we're plotting or something."

"You're probably right," Echo nodded, giving her friend a hug. "Call me if you need me."

"I will," Missy promised.

**

"Good morning, Simon," Echo greeted the trainer with a wan smile.

"Good morning, Echo. I wasn't sure if I'd see you today."

"It feels weird being here, but…anything to take my mind off of…what happened, you know?"

"I hear ya. There's been quite a pall over this place for the past couple of days. How's Joyce?"

"Shaken, but okay."

"Let her know that I asked about her, if you would," Simon's expression was compassionate.

"That's very sweet. I'll let her know. Did Andre have any family in town?"

"Just his cousin Amanda. She worked with him at Chez Vogue. Nobody's seen her for a few days. I'm not even sure she knows what happened yet."

"Oh how awful. I can't even imagine the grief. Andre's poor girlfriend must be devastated," Echo mused, avoiding Simon's eyes for a moment.

"Girlfriend?" Simon's brows shot up his forehead.

"Oh, you know, the brunette with the ponytail who follows him all over the gym," Echo waved her hand breezily.

"Oh, Jenna. She's not a girlfriend, she's more like a groupie," Simon smiled sadly. "Andre was his usual flirtatious self with her, and she took him a little too seriously."

"Understandable. He was quite the charmer," Echo remarked.

"That's what I've heard. All the ladies liked him. Shall we get started?"

"Sure," Echo smiled bravely.

**

"Are we sure that we want to do this?" Missy worried, carrying a hot-out-of-the-oven combination pizza from the best pizza joint in town.

"I did not go through the agony of leg day at the gym only to have you chicken out now. Let's get to the elevator," Echo gestured with the six pack of cola that she was carrying.

"I brought a mini-cooler full of candy bars," Joyce said softly, lifting the cooler for them to see. She'd been unusually quiet lately, so they'd brought her in on their plan in order to take her mind off of what had happened.

"Good thinking. Dessert after pizza," Echo nodded her approval. "Let's go."

She pushed the elevator button and the doors slid silently open on the floor where Chas had the office suite for his Private Investigation Agency. His receptionist, Holly, greeted them with a bright smile. She'd been holding down the fort while Chas and Spencer were gone, and not much had been happening, so she was delighted to see friendly faces in the foyer.

"Hello ladies," she beamed at them from behind her imposing marble desk, professionally dressed as always, even though the boss was away. "Looks like a picnic," she commented, a bit confused.

"Hi Holly," Missy greeted her. "We were hoping that Ringo might be in."

"Really? Uhhh…okay, sure. He's in the "nerve center," doing whatever it is that he does in there. Hold on a sec," she pulled open a file drawer and grabbed a can of air freshener, handing it to Echo. "You might want this," Holly smiled apologetically.

She and Ringo were both important assets to the agency, but the two interacted with each other as seldom as possible. The consummate professional and the disheveled hacker apparently couldn't find much common ground.

"Thanks," Echo was amused, despite the gravity of their situation. She loved the fact that Ringo was unashamedly himself, flying in the face of societal norms, and was brilliant enough to get away with it.

"Down the hall, third door on the left. If it's locked, bang really loudly – he wears headphones quite often."

"Thank you, Holly," Missy smiled at the dignified young lady, wondering just what they were about to encounter.

Joyce, Echo and Missy stood uncertainly outside the door that Holly had indicated, wondering just how to proceed, when it suddenly flew open to reveal a messy-haired, unshaven and rumpled Ringo. The hacker looked at them all one-by-one, confused.

"Is this virtual reality, or am I dreaming?" he ran a hand through his hair. "Three chicks show up with pizza and soda and stuff," he blinked. "Did I order pizza?" He was talking to himself, not them, but Missy answered, taking charge.

"Hi Ringo. I'm Missy, Chas's wife. The girls and I brought you some goodies and we're hoping that you might be able to help us out with finding someone," she explained, handing him the pizza.

"Hmm, I *am* awake. That's cool," he nodded, sniffing the pizza box, as if for confirmation. "Welcome to my lair," he gave them a lopsided grin, then kicked an empty chip bag out of the way so that they could enter a room filled with computers, security screens and various other equipment. While it smelled a bit stale, the room was bearable.

Ringo plopped into a swiveling office chair with the pizza and began eating it as though he hadn't had a meal in days.

"You here about the missing kid in Illinois that Chas is looking for?" he asked, mouth full of pizza.

Echo handed him a soda. "No, actually. We need to find someone else. We only have a first name, but we know where she has a gym membership, and what she looks like."

Ringo popped the tab open on the can of soda, and guzzled half of it in one swift slug, belching afterwards. The look on Joyce's face was priceless as she observed probably the most ill-mannered man she'd ever seen.

"Piece of cake. Probably take me ten minutes to find out anything you'd like to know. Whatcha got in there, gorgeous?" he pointed to the cooler in Joyce's hands, and, unable to even utter a sentence, she handed it over.

"That's how I like 'em, quiet and bearing gifts," he chuckled at his own awful joke, while the three women stared at him. "Candy, awesome. I'll need these after I finish the pizza."

He tossed the cooler aside, grabbed another slice of pizza, stuffing half of it in his mouth in one bite, and setting the remaining half on his knee while he tapped a series of characters into his laptop.

"Okay, what's the name of the gym?" he asked, his words dulled by pizza.

Joyce told him and he tapped it in.

"Hold on, it'll take a sec for me to get past their firewall," his fingers flew across the keyboard, then he stuffed the rest of his piece of pizza in his face and stared at the screen while numbers trailed up and down in a sequence that made no sense to anyone in the room but him.

"Okay, we're in," he swallowed. "Name?"

"Jenna," Echo replied.

"Okay, come to papa, Miss Jenna. Let's see...member photo ID's...here we go," he muttered to himself. "We got four possibilities here," he motioned for them to move closer, and enlarged the four pictures on the screen to show them, then tore the wrapper from one of the candy bars that Joyce had brought.

"That's her," Joyce pointed to the screen.

"Are you sure?" Missy asked.

"Couldn't be more positive. That's the woman who came in and said that she was Andre's girlfriend," the young woman nodded.

"You have a beautiful voice, anyone ever tell you that?" Ringo asked her, licking a flake of chocolate off the back of his hand. Joyce merely stared at him.

"So what do you need to know?" he turned to Echo.

"Everything you can get. Full name, address, occupation, background..."

"Criminal records check," Missy chimed in.

"I gotcha," Ringo nodded. "If you lovely ladies would like to come back in about an hour, I'll have everything you could possibly need and more on Miss Jenna. Oh, and in case you were wondering, there's a burger joint a couple of blocks from here that makes epic burgers and shakes," he hinted.

"We'll see what we can do," Echo smiled faintly at his blatant unspoken request.

"Thank you for your time, Ringo," Missy said, heading for the door.

"Anytime Mrs. B. Come back soon and bring that fine young thing with you," he eyed Joyce.

The trio left without saying another word, leaving the strange genius to his computer magic.

CHAPTER TEN

Missy, Echo and Joyce decided to send Kel back to Chas's office to get the reports from Ringo, armed with two loaded double cheeseburgers, a monster-sized order of fries, and a chocolate shake.

"I hear you're the young man who knows how to get things done around here," Kel barged into the nerve center, bearing his gift of fast food for Ringo.

"Dude, is that from Fat Charlie's?" Ringo asked, apparently not rattled at all by a total stranger bursting into his realm.

"Indeed it is." Kel handed him the large bag of food and the giant shake.

"You bring ketchup and salt?" the hacker inquired, pawing through the bag.

"Naturally. How does one exist without ketchup and salt?"

"Right? That's what I'm talking about," Ringo began tossing fries into his mouth at an alarming speed. Kel merely sat back and waited for the frenzy to slow a bit, so that he could have the young man's undivided attention.

"Whatchu need, bro?" Ringo asked, halfway through his second burger.

"I'm here to collect the information that the three ladies asked you for earlier."

"Yeah, I kinda figure that, since you brought Fat Charlie's and all. I'd offer you a fry, but I think better when I eat, so I'm just gonna eat 'em."

"Not a problem, please, enjoy," Kel smiled. "Were you able to find out anything about our friend Jenna?"

"Chick is all over the place. She must hang out with your ladies a lot."

"What makes you say that?" the artist asked casually.

"I traced her cell phone locator for the last week and tracked her movements," Ringo shrugged.

"Good to know," Kel hid his growing excitement…and concern. "Anything else?"

"She was definitely a gym rat. Spent a ton of time there. She doesn't eat much. Doesn't go out much, other than to hang out with your ladies or the dudes from the gym."

"Which dudes?"

"Andre Weisman, deceased, and Simon Andrews," Ringo took a long pull on his shake, smacking his lips with delight when he swallowed.

"Anything else?"

"She has some odd charges all in one day at a hardware store in the next county. She's not much of a shopper, so it doesn't make sense for her to do all that shopping in one day, in the next county."

"What does she do for a living?"

"Line worker at a factory. Strange job for such a hot chick," Ringo mused.

"I'm assuming you have all of this information in a written report?"

"You got it, my man," Ringo handed over a thick manila envelope.

"Can you print me a recent picture of her?" Kel asked, taking the envelope.

"There are a few of 'em in there already, dude. She's picture worthy," Ringo grinned, slurping down the last dregs of his shake.

"Okay, well, thank you, sir," Kel extended his hand and Ringo shook it.

"No problem, man. Keep me hooked up with Fat Charlie's and I'll tell you anything you wanna know."

**

Phillip "Kel" Kellerman dressed up in jeans and a faded t-shirt for his trip to Mariposa County. He'd be stopping in at the hardware store where Jenna had made her "strange" purchases, according to Ringo.

"G'mornin," the old-timer who was minding the hardware store greeted him. "Coffee's on over by the power tools if you're so inclined."

"Don't mind if I do," Kel mimicked the man's accent almost perfectly. "How are you this mornin?" he asked, heading for the coffee pot, which looked like it contained a fierce, viscous liquid straight from the bowels of the earth, or at least the bottom of a river bed.

"Fair to middlin. My rheumatoid's actin up, makin me thank it's gonna rain. How bout you?"

"Not too dang bad, considerin," Kel continued to play his part. "Got a question for ya," he walked over to the man, with a styrofoam cup of the wicked brew in his hand. "My youngest girl came in here, two-three days ago, and can't remember for the life of her what she bought. She lost the bag of whatever it was and can't find it. Any chance you might remember what she got?"

The old man pursed his lips. "Mebbe," he shrugged. "I seen a lot of folks these past few days."

"This is her," Kel pulled out his wallet, which contained a convincing photo of Jenna that had been cropped to look like a school picture.

"Oh, yep. Purty little thing. Little squirrely, ain't she?" the old man cackled.

"She sure is," Kel chuckled, nodding.

"She came in and got copies of keys. Looked like the originals had been made outta tin or something, so she got good sturdy ones to replace 'em."

"That makes sense," Kel commented. "Say, you don't happen to keep records of the patterns do ya? Those keys were to the doors of my rental properties, and I need the copies."

"Oh, heck yeah. I'll just go to the key impressions for that day and reprint 'em for ya. The computer keeps track of that sorta thing these days."

"I'd appreciate it."

**

"Yep, this one is my shop key," Missy held up one of the keys that Kel had brought home.

"And this one is my studio key," Echo snagged one from the pile.

"And this is my house key," Joyce sighed.

"That leaves three others," Kel observed.

"How are we going to figure out where they're from?" Echo frowned.

"Well, we could try Andre's house," Missy suggested.

"Way too risky," Joyce shook her head vehemently. "The police probably have that place under twenty-four hour surveillance.

"One of them is really small," Echo pointed out, tapping the smallest key with her fingertip.

"That looks like a locker key," Kel commented.

"The gym!" Joyce and Echo exclaimed in unison.

"Jenna must have gotten the master key for the lockers at the gym, and that's how she made imprints of our keys," Echo deduced.

"But how would she have gotten my key to the shop?" Missy was baffled.

"I have one on my key ring, remember?" Echo reminded her.

"But why would she have done this to all of us and then killed Andre?"

"To set us up," Joyce answered without hesitation.

"Could someone really be that obsessed?"

"One way to find out," Kel said, thinking.

"How?" Echo was almost afraid of his answer.

"I'm going to go talk to her. I've been meaning to get in shape for a while. I'll just happen to be working out when she comes in, and I'll strike up a conversation with her."

"And just ask her if she stalked all of us and then killed her boyfriend?" Joyce was skeptical.

"No. I'll just ask her some normal "making conversation" questions and see how she responds."

"Don't you think that she'll know who you are, if she was stalking your wife?"

"I don't know, but what I do know is that we've got to find out what makes her tick, or more to the point, what makes her kill, before more bodies pile up," Kel gave Joyce a pointed look. "If this Andre was interested in you, and she found out about it, you could be in grave danger, young lady."

Joyce nodded. "Okay. Give it a shot, I guess," she said quietly.

CHAPTER ELEVEN

Kel headed for Betty's Diner, a Calgon favorite among the locals, after perusing Jenna's cell phone locator data and seeing that she had frequented the diner up until about a week ago, typically around eleven o'clock every day. He waited until about ten minutes after eleven, to give her time to arrive and get seated, then walked in the door of the old-fashioned eatery. The lunch crowd hadn't yet started to arrive, and the last stragglers from breakfast had finished their coffee and moved on, so there were only a few patrons. His heart leapt a bit when he saw that one of them was Jenna. Taking a seat at the counter, one spot away from her, he beckoned Betty, the iron-haired and iron-willed owner, over.

"Little early for lunch, aren't ya?" she challenged, pouring coffee without having to be asked. She knew her customer's habits and preferences well, and Kel had been coming to the diner since he was a teenager.

"I just couldn't wait to see you," he teased, thanking her for the coffee.

"Uh-huh," Betty rolled her eyes. "The usual or the Special?" she asked, not bothering to use an order pad.

"What's the Special?"

"Mac and Cheese with four cheeses and bacon, with a side of buttered collard greens and a slab of cornbread."

"I think I just heard my arteries harden," Kel chuckled. "I'll take it."

"An extra hour on the treadmill wouldn't hurt you anyway, old man," Betty grumbled good-naturedly as she headed toward the kitchen.

"Ouch, that hurts," Kel put a hand over his heart dramatically.

"It's really good," Jenna spoke up next to him, pointing at her plate.

"Looks like it. I have to indulge my inner carb addict every now and again," he chuckled, glad that she had opened up conversation so that he didn't have to.

"Me too," she sighed, looking glum and picking pieces from her cornbread, dropping them onto her plate.

"You okay?" Kel's voice was soft. "You seem a little sad, if you don't mind my saying so."

"Sorry, I didn't realize it showed that much. I am sad. My boyfriend passed recently, and I just haven't been able to pull it together, you know?"

"Oh, I'm so sorry. I can't even imagine what it would be like to lose my wife. I'd be lost," he commented, making sure to mention a wife so that the young woman at his side wouldn't think that he was hitting on her.

"Exactly," she nodded. "The worst part of it is that I lost all of my pictures and texts from him, so I can't even look at them for the memories."

Kel frowned. "How did that happen? Was there a fire or something?"

Jenna shook her head. "No, I lost my phone a few days before he..." she stopped speaking and took a breath, composing herself. "I must have forgotten my purse somewhere, so everything was gone...my phone, my keys, all of my ID. Like that's what I need to be dealing with right now, when I can't even think straight."

"How awful for you," Kel murmured, his mind busily calculating the logistics of the murder.

"I'm sorry, I didn't mean to bring you down with my business," Jenna stared down at her plate, then looked back up at Kel. "You just have one of those faces that make you seem really easy to talk to."

"I think part of being human is listening when one of our fellow humans needs a good ear, no worries," he replied, meaning it.

"Eat up, buttercup," Betty ordered, sliding Kel's overloaded plate in front of him. "It ain't nearly as good when it's cold."

"Thanks for lunch, Betty. I'd better get going," Jenna tucked money under the edge of her plate, then turned to Kel. "Thanks for listening," she said, and slipped out the door.

"Poor kid," Betty mused, surprising Kel. Betty was usually tough as nails and heartily supported the theory that one should just handle whatever life threw their way, with a stiff upper lip and a healthy dose of pragmatism.

"You know her?"

"Nah, but she's a regular. Didn't come around much last week. I wondered what happened."

"Do you have any idea what happened to the boyfriend?"

"Nope, but I do know that a couple of weeks ago, a guy came in with a black-haired girl, and the gal who just left looked like she could spit nails. She stopped by their table and there were some definite daggers going back and forth between the ladies. The guy looked like he just thought it was funny. Not a very nice boyfriend if you ask me, but who knows with kids these days," Betty confided.

"Yeah, who knows," Kel feigned disinterest. "Makes you wonder who the black-haired girl is."

"I think they work together. When I brought their lunch over, they were talking about inventory or something," Betty shrugged. "You need a box for the rest of that, lightweight?" she nodded at the remaining half of his lunch.

"Yep. I'll have to hide it in my office fridge so that my wife doesn't see my culinary transgression," he grinned and patted his stomach.

"You ain't the first to go astray at my counter," she grabbed the plate, suppressing a smile at her own joke.

**

"Andre worked with a black-haired woman at Chez Vogue. When I talked to Simon right after he was murdered, Simon mentioned that she was his cousin and that no one had seen her since the murder," Echo volunteered, when Kel related his trip to the diner to her, Missy and Joyce.

"Somehow that timing sounds like it might be more than coincidental. Who is Simon?" Kel asked.

"One of the other trainers at the gym. Do you think we should go take Ringo some junk food and get him to try to track down the black-haired girl at Chez Vogue?"

"That's exactly what I was thinking. Her name is Amanda, I remember Andre calling her that when she brought us our tea," Missy added.

"Kel?" Echo looked at her husband hopefully, not really wanting to enter Ringo's lair again.

"Yes, beloved, I will be the deliverer of Fat Charlie's to Mr. Ringo," he chuckled. "The dear boy asked me to order extra pickle next time."

Joyce rolled her eyes. "Beggars can't be choosers," she muttered.

"Whatever Ringo wants, Ringo gets if it helps us solve this thing," Missy reminded her.

"I want him to do more tracking of Jenna's cell phone as well. I'm thinking that it may just lead us to Amanda," Kel mused.

"Huh? How would tracking Jenna's phone lead us to Amanda?" Joyce raised her eyebrows.

"Because Jenna contends that her cell phone was stolen a few days before the murder."

"So, whoever has the cell phone…" Missy began.

"Is the one who has been stalking us all," Echo finished.

"And the one who murdered Andre," Joyce summed up.

"Precisely. If you ladies will excuse me, I'm off to purchase a bag full of grease, salt and other delights," Kel stood and kissed his wife.

"Don't you touch those fries," Echo called after him.

SUMMER PRESCOTT

CHAPTER TWELVE

"These results are puzzling..." Kel surveyed the latest report that he'd gotten from Ringo, with Missy and Echo gazing over his shoulder.

"How so?" Missy asked.

"The cell phone records indicate that Amanda has been all over Calgon, but there's no record of her being at her own apartment."

"Well, that's not so strange," Echo remarked. "If I had a stolen cell phone which might implicate me in a murder, I wouldn't take it home either. She probably has a place that she stashes it before she goes home."

"I just wonder why Ringo couldn't find any other records of her whereabouts, like credit card receipts, ATM withdrawals, things like that. Aside from the cell phone movement, it's like she just disappeared," Kel frowned.

"Don't you think that disappearing is exactly what a murderer would want to do?" Missy pointed out reasonably. "Maybe we should go take a look at her apartment. Talk to her neighbors, see if she's been around."

"Let's wait until we hear back from Ringo. He had a few other sources that he was going to be checking," Kel suggested.

"It's just so frustrating to not know what's going on, particularly with that silly detective looking suspiciously at Missy and Joyce."

"I know, my love, but sometimes patience pays off. When does Chas get back?" he asked Missy.

"Not soon enough," she sighed. "He's on the verge of a break in the kidnapping case down in Illinois, so I can't ask him to come home right now."

"This address seems familiar," Echo murmured, running a fingertip down the list of locator pinpoints. "Kel, will you look it up on your phone?"

"Certainly."

They stared at him, waiting, while his phone took its time loading the info.

"Ah, here we are. Well, that's why it seems familiar," his eyebrows shot up his forehead.

"Why?" Missy asked.

"Because it's the very gym that Echo goes to."

The friends looked at each other.

"So…Jenna lied about losing her phone?" Echo suggested.

"Or maybe Amanda goes to the same gym?" Missy guessed.

"A gym membership wasn't on the list of things that Ringo pulled up for Amanda, but I guess we won't know the answer to all of this until we can locate her."

"Why don't we follow Jenna?" Missy suggested. "Since we don't know where Amanda is, we can follow Jenna around while Ringo tracks her cell phone and see if her activities match up with where her cell phone is."

"How are we going to do that without Sloppy Solinsky catching us?" Echo asked.

"Good point," Kel nodded. "Who do we know that wouldn't be tailed?"

"What about Ringo?" Missy asked.

Echo snorted. "Does Ringo even have a car?"

"He doesn't exactly blend into a crowd, even if he did have a car," Kel pointed out.

"Okay, then what about Holly?"

"She doesn't seem like the amateur private investigator type," Echo made a face.

"She works for a P.I., and besides, she's relatively the same age as Jenna, and is young and fit. It would make sense for her to be in some of the same places."

"You do have a point," Kel nodded.

"So, who's going to persuade her to leave her cushy office job in order to follow a potential murderer around?" Echo blinked at Missy.

"Missy's request would carry the most weight since Holly works for Chas," Kel said reasonably.

"Okay," Missy sighed. "I'll ask. At least I can bring cupcakes rather than fast food as a means of encouragement."

"Does she even eat cupcakes?" Echo asked. "I would think that she'd have a very strict eating regimen."

"I guess there's only one way to find out."

**

"Good afternoon, Mrs. Beckett. How are you today?" Holly's greeting was courteous and professional, as always.

"I'm fine, thank you, Holly, and please, call me Missy. I brought you some cupcakes," she set the pink box on the counter. "I've been trying lots of new recipes while Chas has been gone."

"Oh," the receptionist looked at the box, but didn't touch it. "How thoughtful," she smiled.

There was an awkward moment of silence while Missy desperately grasped for something to say, not knowing how to lead into a conversation where she was going to ask her husband's receptionist to follow a murderer.

"Keeping busy?" she asked, kicking herself for how lame she sounded.

"Absolutely," Holly frowned. "I've been working really hard to organize the cold-case files that Mr. Beckett left for me. Just because he's away doesn't mean that I haven't been diligently…" she began earnestly.

Missy put up a hand to stop her. "I know, don't worry, I didn't mean anything by that. I was just making conversation. I know you're very good at your job, Chas is quite pleased with your work," she assured the serious young woman, wishing that she'd sent Kel to take care of this task.

"Look, I'm just going to be very honest with you. I have a…project that I need help with, and I'm hoping that you might be able to lend a hand. You'd be paid, of course."

"Oh?"

"Yes, I uh…well, it's sort of private investigation work," Missy began.

"Oh, I'm not certified for that," Holly shook her head.

"I know, and you don't need to be. It's not actually P.I. work, it just might…feel like it."

"I'm sorry, Mrs. Beckett, I'm afraid I don't understand."

"Holly, I'm going to tell you some things in confidence, and I want you to understand that I'd never ask you to do anything that was wrong or illegal," Missy opened the box of cupcakes and started eating one. Cupcakes and talking just went naturally together, it was a habit…or an occupational hazard.

"I believe that I may have identified the suspect in a recent homicide," she began.

Holly's eyes widened. "Really? That's so amazing. I bet the police were grateful."

"Uh, no. The police don't know. They think that I'm a person of interest in the case. That's why I need your help."

Holly looked decidedly uncomfortable, but Missy continued, before she could say anything.

"There is a young woman who claimed to be the victim's girlfriend, and I've uncovered a tremendous amount of evidence that points to her being the perpetrator." Missy couldn't bring herself to use the word killer.

"All that I would need you to do is follow her movements for a couple of days. Write down where she goes and when. You'd never have to have any contact with her at all."

"Why do the police consider you to be a person of interest?"

"Because apparently, the victim had taken a bite of one of my cupcakes before he died, so they think that I might have been somehow involved in his death."

Holly's eyes flicked to the box on the counter next to her, then to the half-eaten cupcake in Missy's hand.

"Who would run the office while I was out?" Holly surprised her by asking.

A little jolt of hope ran through her as she realized that at least the young woman was considering the possibility.

"We'd just close it down for a couple of days. There aren't any clients coming in while Chas and Spencer are gone anyway."

"What about Ringo?"

"He'd still have access if he needed it."

"Would I get overtime?"

"Absolutely."

"Would I be done at a reasonable hour at night?"

"You can be in bed by nine if you'd like."

"And it's just for a couple of days and there's nothing illegal going on?"

"Exactly."

"Okay," the young woman nodded, surprising Missy again by taking a cupcake and nibbling at it. "What do I need to know about this girl?"

CHAPTER THIRTEEN

Amanda Bernsen, Andre Weisman's cousin, had stolen a suitcase-sized amount of designer clothing, and an equally large amount of fine jewelry from Chez Vogue over the course of the past few weeks, never taking more than a piece or two at a time. She knew just which areas of the store weren't monitored by security cameras, and at which angles to position her body so that she could pilfer items without being caught. She had access to all of this knowledge as a result of bringing one particular security guard lunch every day for a few weeks.

After pawning the jewelry at various shops outside of Calgon, the enterprising young thief had left the job one day without notice, never to return. She'd hitchhiked her way out of Florida, and with the money from the pawned jewelry, had been working her way up the East coast, stealing wherever she could, and getting away with it because her fine designer clothes made her look as though she belonged in the various boutiques where she scored her bounty.

Amanda stayed in hotels that were nice enough to have a wealthy clientele, and found that even many of the richest were still naïve enough to put their wallets in their back pockets. She rationalized her behavior, believing that she was doing them a favor by teaching them to be more careful in the future, and she was having an exhilarating time doing it.

"May I?" an older gentleman, with a finely tailored suit, gestured to the spot next to her at the counter of the well-appointed mahogany bar.

"Please," she smiled, imitating the social graces of her long-dead mother.

"Sure is hot out there," he blotted away the moisture that the Carolina sun and humidity had inflicted upon his brow.

"Nice and cool in here," she purred, recognizing a mark when she saw one.

"You from these parts?"

"No sir, I'm a Yankee," she simpered. "On my way home after a lovely holiday."

"Well, I'd like to show you a little southern hospitality and buy you a drink," he offered. "What'll you have?"

"Surprise me," Amanda flirted. "I'll be right back, I have to powder my nose," she winked at him and climbed down from her barstool, brushing against him on the way down. "Oh, excuse me," she pretended to be embarrassed. "I'm so clumsy."

"You're also under arrest," the man said gravely, securing her arms behind her in a flash. "I watched you steal three wallets with that move last night, but couldn't get to you fast enough. Now you've stolen mine and you're going to jail."

When the southern gentleman, who was actually an undercover cop, finished tightening her handcuffs, a uniformed officer approached and led her away, reading her rights as they walked.

**

Holly had dressed casually for her assignment, donning denim shorts, comfortable sandals, and a breathable tank top. In that outfit, she could run if she had to, and she'd be comfortable going into most establishments if her surveillance had to be done on foot. Missy had told her to just stay in her car, but if the suspect went somewhere on foot, Holly wasn't about to take a chance on losing her. She might not be certain about the wisdom of accepting this assignment, but by golly since she had committed to it, she was determined to do it right.

She'd waited in the neighborhood outside of Jenna's house, until she saw the young woman leave. Giving her enough of a lead so as not to be noticed, Holly pulled smoothly out into traffic, never losing sight of the young woman. Apparently having a particular talent for not looking conspicuous, she had a smoothie at the bar in the gym while Jenna worked out, read the paper on a park bench while Jenna jogged, and stocked up on dry goods while Jenna grocery shopped. She wanted to go into the diner for lunch when Jenna stopped there, but didn't dare because the venue looked too small for her to come in without being noticed.

Using a digital voice recorder so that she never had to take her hands from the wheel while driving, Holly diligently noted the precise time of Jenna's every move, making certain to repeat each time distinctly, twice. At first, the assignment had been fun, but, since Jenna seemed to have a very ordinary existence, which involved an inordinate amount of time spent sitting in the car for Holly, the initial charm wore thin.

Jenna had gone to a non-descript grey cinder-block building after lunch, where Holly presumed she worked. The small plaque on the door, as seen through the zoom function of her cell phone camera, said simply *A & E Model Works*. Was Jenna a model? It would make sense, given her youth and fitness level, despite having a rather non-remarkable appearance. Holly did a quick search on her phone and found that *A & E Model Works* was actually a processing plant which churned out plastic parts for snap-together model planes, cars, and other vehicles to delight hobbyists.

"Oh boy," she sighed, leaning her head against the window of her car. "Even her job is boring. She probably killed the guy just to break the monotony."

After sitting across the street from *A & E* for three hours, her stomach protesting loudly at the lack of food, because she'd finished her bagged lunch hours earlier and had run out of snacks, Holly texted Missy to see if it would be okay for her to go grab a bite of dinner from a nearby taco stand. Of course, Missy told her to go ahead, so she got an order of shrimp tacos to go and came back to her nicely shaded parking spot to eat.

"It's a picnic," she commented optimistically, biting into the tender, spicy taco and savoring the combination of flavors.

Around nine o'clock, when Holly was starting to get more than a little drowsy, and had to pee so badly that she thought she'd burst, Jenna and a handful of her coworkers emerged from the building.

"Quitting time," Holly murmured, waiting to start her car until some of the others did as well, so that she wouldn't call attention to herself. When Jenna's car left the lot, she waited until three other cars fell in behind her before pulling out into the road and doing a u-turn to follow.

"She's going home, what a surprise," Holly yawned.

Missy had told her that she could call it a day anytime that she wanted, but she had a hunch that when Jenna went home for the evening, she might not stay there. After all, most crimes happened at night, and she didn't want to miss any activity that might be significant.

There was a gas station just a couple of blocks from Jenna's house, and when Holly couldn't stand it anymore, she drove there for a bathroom break, grabbing coffee and a bag of trail mix while she was there. When she came back to her observation post up the street from Jenna's home, she noted that a car had pulled up on the side street closest to her. Recording the make and model, because she couldn't see the color very well, she watched a figure exit the vehicle and head for the alley behind Jenna's house.

"What's this all about?" she whispered, her heart beating faster.

She texted Missy to see what she should do, but received no answer. Deducing that Missy was probably asleep, she was left to figure out her next move on her own. The lights were on in what looked like Jenna's living room, kitchen and upstairs bedroom, and when all were extinguished simultaneously, instinct made Holly's decision for her. Heart thundering in her chest and adrenalin crashing through her veins, she slipped silently from her car and hurried toward the alley behind Jenna's house, where the dark figure had gone.

**

Timothy Eckels had been busy from the time that his feet hit the floor. There had been a rash of deaths overnight, completely coincidental and not of a suspicious nature, and he and Fiona had been tagging and bagging all day. Summer was like that sometimes. He wondered if folks just got tired of fighting the heat. When he sank into his desk chair after a ridiculously long day, he opened his email, and the first item that caught his attention was the toxicology report on Andre Weisman.

Clicking on it, he scanned it first, looking for specific things, then nodding, he went back and reread it to make certain that he had seen what he thought he saw. Fiona appeared in the doorway, stifling a yawn.

"Hey boss-man, are we done yet?" she sighed, leaning against the door frame.

"I was right," he looked up, eyebrows raised, ignoring her question entirely.

From the look on his face, she knew that their long day had just gotten longer.

"About what?" she perked up a bit.

"The poison. I know what it is now, and while it was the same poison that was used on the cupcake, it wasn't delivered by the cupcake. It was ingested in a liquid form."

"Just like you thought," Fiona nodded. "Want me to get Detective Dufus on the phone?"

Tim shook his head, thinking. "I'd rather not, but I suppose we have no choice. Go ahead, call him."

**

Art Solinsky hates it when crime happens after five o'clock. If his work phone rings after quitting time, it automatically puts him in a bad mood. When he saw the Coroner's number appear on his screen after eight o'clock, he grimaced and considered not picking up, but decided to cover his bases and see what the creepy undertaker wanted.

"Solinsky," he barked into the phone.

He listened for a few minutes, his sour expression growing darker by the minute.

"You called me at this hour to talk to me about lab results, when you haven't even drawn up a report? What were you thinking, Eckels? The guy ain't gonna be any less dead if you wait until morning to send over my report," Solinsky grumbled before hanging up.

**

Timothy Eckels stared at the phone in his hand, speechless for a moment.

"Well, that went well," Fiona rolled her eyes. "Now what?"

"If Solinsky isn't interested in catching a killer, I know who will be. Get me Chas Beckett," the Coroner replied grimly.

Fiona dialed the number, listened to a recorded message, and pushed End on her phone, frustrated.

"Chas Beckett is out of town. Any suggestions?"

"Call Melissa Beckett and see if she knows how to get in touch with him."

"It's that important?" Fiona hesitated.

"There's a killer on the loose. Solinsky may not be overly concerned about that, but I will not have blood on my hands because I didn't try," the look on Tim's face was grave.

"Okay," Fiona nodded, looking up Missy's number.

**

Missy and Echo had just come back in from a long walk with Jasmine and the dogs, when Missy's phone rang.

"Timothy Eckels?" she murmured, glancing at the screen. "That can't be good."

"You don't suppose that Holly…?" Echo left the question unfinished, her eyes wide.

"Hello?" Missy answered in a hurry.

"Mrs. Beckett, I'm sorry to bother you so late in the evening, but I would really like to get in touch with your husband, regarding a case that I'm dealing with," Tim explained.

"Oh, I'm sorry, Tim, Chas is out of state at the moment. I know that you're limited as to what you can tell me, but I have to ask…does this have anything to do with the Andre Weisman case?" she blurted.

His silence spoke volumes, so she continued.

"Okay, so I don't know if you know or not, but I'm listed as a person of interest in the case, as is one of my dear friends, so I've been doing a little investigating on my own, because Detective Solinsky just won't listen…" she began in a rush.

"I'm aware of that propensity in the detective," Tim answered dryly, recalling his most recent conversation with Art Solinsky.

"Well, the long and short of it is that I've got a young woman who is following the person that I think is the killer, and if I've put that young woman in danger, then I'd appreciate it if you'd tell me. Did you find a clue during an autopsy or something? Anything that you could tell me would help," Missy pleaded for information, worried about Holly and kicking herself for putting the receptionist potentially in harm's way.

Another moment of silence from Tim, and then, "Is the person that you're following a horticulturalist by chance?"

"I seriously doubt it, why?" Missy was mystified.

Tim told her about his suspicions, and what he'd discovered in the lab results, which didn't really mean much to Missy, but when she related the information to Echo, after hanging up the phone, the blood drained from Echo's face, and she clutched at the handle of Jasmine's stroller.

"I know who the killer is," she whispered.

"Oh no," Missy glanced at her phone, seeing that she had missed multiple messages from Holly while she'd been on the phone with Timothy Eckels. "Tell me quickly, I have to call the police. I think Holly may be in trouble," she worried, her heart skipping a beat.

CHAPTER FOURTEEN

Holly shook with a heady combination of fear and excitement as she stayed within the shadows and crossed into the alley behind Jenna's house. Moving as quietly as she could, she followed the path that the potential intruder had taken, and saw the fuse box for the house with its door hanging open. She briefly considered throwing the breaker back into place and lighting everything up to illuminate the dark figure she'd seen, but didn't want to put Jenna in danger, so she dismissed the thought and continued on, hoping against hope that whoever was out there couldn't hear her.

Crouching behind a bush, she saw the figure, who was quite large, so she assumed that it was a man, doing something at the back door. A few seconds later, the lock on the door released, and the intruder slipped inside.

Thinking that this was way outside the scope of her duties, and tempted to just call 911 and let things work themselves out, Holly instead crept forward, staying low so as not to be detected through the windows. It might take several minutes for the police to arrive, and if she could distract the intruder somehow in the meantime, she might be able to prevent a tragedy from happening. Even if this was just a garden-variety thief, which she doubted, she might be able to scare him off somehow.

Holly was about three feet from the back door, when she heard a soft, hiccupping sound and realized that it was probably Jenna, scared out of her wits and crying. The sound was coming from an upstairs open window, which meant that, most likely, the intruder hadn't gotten to her yet. Wondering how to capture Jenna's attention without alerting the intruder to her presence, Holly quickly decided that creating a diversion might be the best way to go. She could make a noise, then run, drawing the intruder away. She was pretty fast, and would have a head start, so she decided to give the ill-conceived plan a shot.

Bending down, Holly picked up a large rock from beside the back steps and hurled it into the house, hearing it thud loudly against something. She turned to run and was suddenly blinded by a powerful flashlight.

"Calgon Police Department, stop and put your hands over your head! You are under arrest!" a voice came through a bullhorn.

"I'm not who you want, you dimwits!" Holly shouted back, putting her hands up as she was told. "I work for Chas Beckett. The burglar is inside, and the homeowner is trapped," she yelled, fearing for Jenna's safety.

She heard a loud bang behind her, then the sounds of a scuffle as police tackled the intruder. It took several of the officers to contain the intruder, and when they had him on the ground, the pulled off the ski mask that he'd been wearing.

Jenna, who stood back trembling and watching the spectacle in her foyer, gasped at the reveal. "Simon?" she was aghast. "How could you? You killed Andre, I knew it!" she hollered in a rage, charging over as though she wanted to attack him.

She was restrained by two police officers, as the remaining four escorted the bodybuilder to a patrol car.

Art Solinsky hadn't bothered to show up for the "Burglary in Progress" call, made by Melissa Beckett, that had gone out to the police department, so it was the uniformed cops who brought in Andre Weisman's killer.

Holly came up behind Jenna and touched her lightly on the arm, causing her to jump a bit. "Are you okay?" she asked.

Jenna frowned. "Who are you?" Her teeth were still chattering from fear and adrenalin.

"Just someone who was watching out for you," Holly replied quietly.

"I'm fine," Jenna turned away to pay attention to an officer who needed to take a statement, and Holly slipped away into the night.

CHAPTER FIFTEEN

Chas Beckett was astonished at the tale his wife told upon his return.

"So, Eckels called Solinsky with the results and Solinsky brushed him off?" Chas was shook his head in disbelief. "Timothy Eckels doesn't pick up the phone unless he absolutely has to, so if he makes a call, it's important."

"Exactly," Missy nodded. "So, when I told Tim that you were out of town, he sounded a bit upset. I talked to him a little bit more and told him that I was doing a rather unofficial investigation and he told me what he found out when the lab results came in."

"Which was?"

"The poison that was used to kill Andre was Sodium Fluoroacetate, which is derived from plants that only grow certain places in the world. One of the poisonous plants is called a Poison Pea, and it grows in Australia. When I told Echo that, she knew immediately that our culprit was most likely the trainer at the gym who had taken Andre's place. He studied botany and landscaping in college," Missy explained.

"When they searched his house after his arrest, they found lots of the Poison Pea plants potted in pretty containers in his kitchen."

Chas nodded, impressed. "So, what was his motive for killing Andre?" he asked.

"Jealousy."

"He was jealous of Andre's position at the gym? That doesn't seem to be a likely motive for murder."

"Oh no, he was jealous of Andre's attention and affection. He had a crush on him, and Andre had refused his advances, according to some witnesses at the gym, so he set out to bring down every woman he could find whom Andre had flirted with, which is why Echo and Joyce and

Jenna and I were involved. When they arrested Simon at Jenna's house, they found a bag he'd been carrying that he was going to use to plant evidence at her house. She'd made it her mission to make Andre fall in love with her, and Simon couldn't stand it, apparently."

"What evidence was in the bag?"

"Some of the same kind that he'd planted in Joyce's car. Hair samples, clothing fibers, he apparently knew a little bit about police procedure. He had the master key to the lockers at the gym, and used it to steal Jenna's key ring, which had all the copies of keys for me, Joyce and Echo, giving him access. He also stole Jenna's phone, hoping to place the blame on her."

"But why did Jenna have copies of all of your keys?" Chas was confused.

"Because apparently Simon wasn't the only one obsessed with Andre. Jenna had one date with him and thought that he was her boyfriend from then on. She was stalking all of us, but didn't do the damage to Echo's studio, Joyce's house, and my shop. Simon did it, while carrying her cell phone, hoping that it was being tracked so that he could set her up."

"Wow, a man and a woman, obsessed with the same guy. This Andre must've really been something," Chas mused.

"He was very nice," Missy said sadly.

"So about you conducting investigations in my absence," Chas gave his wife a mock-stern look.

"You weren't here," Missy said in a small voice.

"While I admire your initiative and cleverness, you put yourself, Echo, Joyce and one of my employees in danger," he chided her gently, his eyes filled with love and concern.

"I know."

"And now I can't get Holly to stop asking me if she can get certified to become a P.I.," he sighed with a smile.

"I've created a monster?" Missy grinned.

"So it would seem," Chas smiled at his adorable wife.

"Ringo was quite helpful as well."

"Yeah, he told me that he put on a little weight while I was gone, and that some "righteous chicks" had a "dude" bring him goodies in exchange for favors. You wouldn't know anything about that, now would you?"

Missy made a zipping motion across her lips and shook her head.

"What am I going to do with you?" Chas chuckled, taking her into his arms.

"A swim sounds nice," she murmured against his chest, disappointed when his phone rang.

Chas glanced at the screen and answered it.

"Beckett here…I understand…Yes, I will…Yes sir…Thank you," he hung up quickly.

"It's been a while since I was summoned to the Chief's office," he mused, tucking his cell phone into his pocket.

"I spoke with him after the arrest. He apologized to me for Detective Solinsky's behavior and thanked me for the role that I played in apprehending the suspect," Missy beamed proudly.

"That's how you found out all the details. Oh boy, I'm sure I'll hear about that when I talk to him," Chas shook his head, amused.

"I think Timothy Eckels misses you."

"It's a shame that Solinsky treats him badly. Eckels is a real asset to the department," Chas made a face.

"Solinsky treats everyone badly," Missy grimaced, having been eyed with suspicion by the irascible detective on more than one occasion.

"I feel for the Chief, this can't be making his job any easier," Chas sighed.

"Well, go talk to the man. He'll probably appreciate your input."

"Not much for me to do at this point – the murderer is in jail, but I'll be happy to go talk about it."

"Hurry back, I'll put on my swim suit," Missy batted her eyes.

"I'll be back in record time," Chas promised, with a kiss on the tip of her nose.

"Good, because Echo made me buy a bikini while you were gone," she winked.

"I knew I liked that gal," Chas chuckled on his way out the door.

CHAPTER SIXTEEN

Spencer Bengal, the young Marine veteran who had gone from being Chas Beckett's bodyguard to working for him as a junior P.I., had a heavy heart this evening, for lots of reasons. His on-again-off-again girlfriend, famous horror writer Izzy Gilmore, had moved back to New York, without warning, and he hadn't heard from her since. All of his calls and texts had been ignored. He knew that she was alive and well, he'd tracked her trips and expenditures, not to stalk her, but just to know that she was okay. He'd been dismayed to find that when he returned from Illinois, the cozy pink cottage, that she'd bought when she moved to Calgon, had a For Sale sign in front of it.

Spencer's only wish was that she'd be happy, though it hurt to finally admit that they just weren't the right match for each other. He'd continue to enjoy her company through the words of her books, and would cheer her successes from afar.

What weighed most heavily on the young man's heart this evening was the suffering of his friend and former brother-at-arms, Janssen, whose real name, he'd discovered, was Will Channing. The two had served together in a covert program in Afghanistan, and had weathered some pretty chilling circumstances together, working for the government in a secret capacity.

Janssen had spent the last year, since the two came back from combat, trying to acclimate to civilian life, and finding it nearly impossible. He'd lived off of the land for a year, since the two came back from combat, trying to acclimate to civilian life, and finding it nearly impossible. He'd lived off the land and stayed out of sight of humans for the most part, trying to work through the nightmares and pain of the past.

When he'd at last worked up the courage to approach his wife and thirteen year old son, who had been told by the government that he was dead, he didn't receive quite the reception that he'd hoped, which caused him to seriously doubt whether or not he'd ever be able to function in polite society, or the intimate realm of a family. It was obvious that Janssen loved his wife and son so profoundly that it hurt, but the question plaguing him now was whether or not love was enough to bridge the gap that had been caused by governmentally mandated deception.

Spencer had encouraged his friend to come back to Calgon with him, hoping that he could help him work through his emotions, as well as allowing Janssen's wife the space that she'd requested. From the way he'd described it to Spencer, Rossalyn Channing had looked like she'd seen a ghost when her husband, whose empty casket she'd buried nearly a year ago, appeared.

Spencer lived in a guest house at the back of the estate that Missy and Chas had recently purchased and renovated, so that he could provide an extra measure of security for the heir of the Beckett family fortune. Janssen would be staying with him there, indefinitely, and would be helping out at Chas's agency to earn his keep.

He slept on the floor, not having been able to become accustomed to sleeping in a bed again, after surviving some harrowing experiences in the Middle East, and often went for long treks during the middle of the night, when nightmares as fresh as blood on a battleground haunted him. Every creak of the house settling, every groan of the wind making the palm trees sway and the palmetto leaves skitter against each other, put him on full alert, his keen senses attuned to every sound and scent.

Spencer was going to try his best to help ease Janssen back into real life, and was hoping that he could find a compassionate professional who would help him out. In the meantime, he'd give his friend the space that he needed, and would pretend not to notice the swollen redness of his eyes after yet another sleepless and tearful night.

One of the things that he'd be using to try to get Janssen's mind off of his misery, was a serial killer case that he wanted to wrap up personally. Timothy Eckels' wife a notorious killer, and she'd been nearly within Spencer's grasp twice and slipped through his fingers. With

Janssen's help, he was determined to find her and bring her in so that justice would finally be done.

CHAPTER SEVENTEEN

"Check it out, Timmy," Fiona shoved the morning paper under her boss's nose. "You're a hero."

"I don't read newspapers," the mortician said mildly, blinking at her.

"I know. You don't read newspapers, you don't watch the news, you don't listen to the radio, I get it. You've got to let go of her," she said earnestly, referring to the specter of his wife and the horrors she'd committed. "What she did wasn't your fault, and you shouldn't let her keep you in emotional prison for the rest of your life," Fiona asserted, eyebrows raised, hands on hips.

"This is a workplace, and your comments are entirely inappropriate," his mask slammed firmly into place.

"Yeah, they always are. Especially when they involve something that scares you to your foundations," she tossed the paper on the desk in front of him. "The Chief of Police had some good things to say about you. You should be proud," she stared at the top of his head because he steadfastly refused to meet her gaze. "Somebody other than me should be anyway," she muttered, and slipped quietly out of the room.

**

"I know that you're in private practice right now, Chas, but I could sure use you around here," the Chief pulled no punches.

"What about Solinsky?"

"One more strike and he's out. I've got a paper trail a mile long on his incompetence. It borders on dereliction of duty. Between you, me and the fence post, if there's one more screw up, he gets his walking papers. I'll need somebody working homicide while I find a replacement, and you're the man I'd like to see on the job," the Chief shrugged.

"My presence here would cause a great deal of friction with Solinsky," Chas said carefully, not committing to anything.

"Good, maybe he'll leave and I won't have to fire him."

"Using me as an irritant, Chief?" Chas smirked.

"No, using you as the best homicide detective I've ever worked with, bar none. If that also happens to help me get rid of Solinsky, I'm certainly not opposed to the idea," the Chief's mouth twitched in amusement.

"I do have an extra guy at the agency right now, which will free up some of my time," Chas mused.

"I'm not asking you to come back permanently, although that door is absolutely open, I just need your help during Solinsky's transition out, and the new detective's transition in. Can you help me out?"

"Before I can give you an answer, I do need to discuss it with Missy."

"Of course, I'd expect nothing less. Talk to her, chew on it a little bit, and let me know – the sooner the better."

"Will do," Chas nodded. "Eckels came through again," he commented.

"The guy is an odd duck, but he's a genius when it comes to pulling clues from the stiffs. I got the city council to approve a raise for him, but he turned it down."

"What? Why?" Chas frowned.

"Said that he'd rather have the money in the form of a scholarship so that his assistant can go to mortuary school."

"So there's a pretty generous guy hiding under that lab coat and glasses," Chas nodded. "I suspected as much."

"He and Solinsky are like oil and water," the Chief shook his head.

"From what I understand, Solinsky has that effect on folks," Chas stood to go.

"Good seeing you again, Beckett. Think about what I said and let me know," the Chief shook his hand.

"You'll know as soon as I do," Chas promised.

CHAPTER EIGHTEEN

"I'm so glad that you were able to join us this morning, Joyce," Missy beamed, placing a steaming cup of coffee and a tray of cupcakes in front of the young woman.

"It sure beats going to the gym," Joyce joked.

It had taken her a few weeks to get over being stalked and the reality of Andre's death, but she had bounced back and decided that she was better suited to the curvy lifestyle.

"You and Echo do this every morning?" she was astonished.

"Just about," Echo grinned. "Coffee and cupcakes are a great way to start the day."

"No wonder you're always in such a good mood," Joyce grinned. "Missy, I'm a baker from way back, and these have to be the best cupcakes I've ever had," she enthused, slowly chewing a bite of nutty fudge cupcake.

"Thanks, I'm glad you like them. Join us anytime," she invited.

"I heard that Spencer was back in town," Joyce tried to sound casual, but the rising blush beneath her mocha skin gave her away.

"He is, but he's dealing with a breakup, so give him some space," Echo warned.

"You know what guys dealing with a breakup need? My home cooking, that's what," Joyce asserted.

"He did rave about your cooking," Missy nodded.

"See," Joyce said triumphantly, taking another bite of cupcake.

"Just take it slowly," Echo cautioned, ever-protective.

Spencer had helped her start her candle-making business by sitting with her and dipping candles for hours. The young man held a special place in her heart, and while she thought that he and Joyce would make a great couple, she knew that he was dealing with emotional issues of his own.

"Honey, after that last mess at the gym, I'll take it anyway that I can get it," Joyce wisecracked. "I gotta get going so that we can open up on time. Can I get a to-go cup?" she asked, holding up her mug of coffee.

"You betcha," Missy popped up from her seat to grab a cup.

"Whew," Echo breathed, after Joyce left. "Maybe now we'll all have a chance to catch our breath."

"I sure hope so. Chas is going to be spending more time at the station for a while, so we'll have lots of chances for girl time, and I'd love to include Joyce – she's a hoot!"

"Yes, she is. I'm lucky I found her. She runs the bookstore and candle shop single-handedly most of the time."

"Is your studio up and running again?"

"Thankfully, yes," Echo's expression was thoughtful for a moment.

"Uh-oh…" Missy stared at her best friend. "I know that look…what are you up to, young lady?"

"Nothing," Echo widened her eyes in mock-innocence. "I just think that Spencer and Joyce could make an awfully cute couple," she grinned devilishly, then took a sip of her coffee.

"You stop it," Missy chided. "Leave that boy alone. Let nature take care of things."

"Sometimes nature needs a little encouragement."

"What about telling Joyce to take it slow?" Missy challenged.

"Oh, that was just me trying to sound responsible."

"You're incorrigible."

"That's why we're friends."

Copyright 2017 Summer Prescott Books

All Rights Reserved